BILL VAN PARYS

The
NIGHT THING
and other Tales of
GLOOM AND DOOM

AuthorHouse™
1663 Liberty Drive
Bloomington, IN 47403
www.authorhouse.com
Phone: 833-262-8899

This book is printed on acid-free paper.

ISBN: 978-1-6655-1088-2 (sc)
ISBN: 978-1-6655-1089-9 (e)

Print information available on the last page.

Published by AuthorHouse 12/12/2020

authorHOUSE®

The
NIGHT THING
and other Tales of
GLOOM AND DOOM

Contents

The Night Thing

by
William Van Parys III

The reports had been coming in from around the Phoenix area on and off throughout January 1996. Reports of some strange shadowy creature that no one had really gotten a good look at. It had been described as being between 6 and 7 feet tall with, some said anyway, a cat like head with unusually large fangs, two or more tentacles like arms with huge paw like hands and extraordinarily long claws that were barbed at the ends. In addition to this the legs were more bird or chicken like with claws protruding from them. The eyes again cat like but the pupils were horizontal slits, black in color, the rest of the eyes a sick looking green that seemed to glow just slightly.

The first sightings had come from several eyewitnesses from the Sun City area. A 57 your old resident named Greta Joyce had been out one very early morning to pick up the daily paper when it had come out of the bushes in her front yard. She said it looked as if it wanted to attack her when a splash of headlights across the lawn had frightened it away. Greta immediately went in and dialed 911 for the police to relate her insane story to the apparently bored officer on duty.

The conversation went like this word for word:

Greta: HELP!!! There's something in my front yard. I think it wanted to attack me. PLEASE!!! You've got to send the police right away, HURRY!!!

Dispatcher: Your area code please.

Greta: What the fuck does it matter, just get the police here now, HURRY!!!

Dispatcher: (voice soothing) Please you've got to calm down. Now I need your area code please. (She was beginning to gain some interest this lady did not seem like a wacko to her.)

Greta: (Deep but shaky breath and in a fairly calm voice she began to explain everything, starting with the area code.) At about 4:30 this morning I got up and went outside to get the morning paper and when I bent down to pick it up the bushes in front of me started to rattle. When I looked up I saw this thing right out of a nightmare I tell you.

Dispatcher: Ma'am I've dispatched a squad car to your home. The officer is going to need a description when he gets there. Right now I have all I needthank you. Goodbye. (Click.)

Greta had started to say something but the dispatcher had cut her off before she started. She said to no one if particular (since she lived alone for going on 5 years now since her husband Earl had died of a heart attack) "I guess now all I have to do is wait for the cops."

Greta really did not want to wait here alone all by her lonesome waiting for either the cops or that thing to come back. That latter thought sent a chill up her spine that gave her the chills that did not subside until lights from the squad car splashed up her driveway.

The widow Greta Joyce gave the best available description of the "Night Thing" (as it was dubbed by the papers throughout the month of January) to this date, January 27, 1996.

The next sighting (by 2 crack heads) was on the corner of Buckeye and 10th St. at about 1am. The 2 "tweekers" said they were just sitting minding their own business when across the street they saw one of the shadows move. It didn't actually move, rather something darker colored than the shadow itself started to come out of the darkness and into the light.

The creature according to we'll call him, tweeker #1 was actually darker than black itself. More accurately light seemed to be swallowed up by its darkness. It then appeared to be thinking of attacking them. Realizing they might be in danger they got the hell out of there. A mile of running later they encountered a police car and spilled their story to the 2 cops on patrol. That was on the night of January 3, 1996.

As the night of January 6th turned into the morning of January 7th young Freddy Johnson's (nicknamed "Slice-Em-Freddy") mother began to get seriously worried about her son. He usually strolled in around midnight, after all the was only sixteen. He always came home however, and it was now pushing 7am. He'd been expelled again so school was not a problem, although Anna Johnson (his mom) wanted him to get a job to help pay the bills. It wasn't like "Slice-Em-Freddy" not to show up at all and by noon January 8th, Anna Johnson reported Freddy missing.

Frederick "Slice-Em-Freddy" Johnson was a lowly street punk if there ever was one. His nickname was derived from the time he got his first Butterfly knife. While learning to use it he slashed the palm of his left hand, his friends saw this and started to call him "Sliced" he hated that nickname and it finally evolved into "Slice-Em-Freddy". He liked that and he felt it had a nice ring to it. His heritage was half Cuban on his mother's side, and half white mostly Irish on his dad's side. Freddy was proud of his Cuban heritage because his mother was "too cool" and his father would beat him up. His father would get drunk, accuse Freddy of hanging around with a bunch of niggers and wet backs and would commence to smacking Freddy, and even his mother around for a while. After that he would get even more drunk and simply pass out.

Meril Johnson (Freddy's dad) was killed one night when he tried to rob a liquor store on Indian School Road. He didn't, nor could he have, known there were three police officers around back who were rounding up vagrants and drunks to take down to the county jail. They heard Meril Johnson shoot and kill the clerk. They ran around to the front of the building, saw Meril, told him to drop the gun, and Meril then shot the first cop to arrive at the front of the building. He shot him in the right knee severing the main artery, causing doctors to amputate his leg just above the knee so he would not bleed to death. The other two officers then shot Meril to death.

Around midnight of January 6th, "Slice-Em-Freddy" was just getting ready to go home when he decided to walk down an alley not too far from home. He needed to take a whizz something fierce. There he was pissing out all the beer he'd been drinking when he saw a shadow just out of the corner of his eye. Thinking it was one of his gang just screwing around he yelled "Hey asshole, you wanna knock that shit off, I got my knife you know." No answer. He was feeling uneasy for some reason and he didn't know why. He pulled his butterfly knife out and got ready for battle (something he'd gotten used to). Silence, nothing but. He waited, more than a little alert now. Without warning something too black to reflect light, fell upon him so fast he didn't even have time to react. With one swipe of its claw the thing ripped his right arm off at the shoulder and before he could scream it tore off his head. With that done it began to dine.

There were no reports or encounters for almost a week, when about 1am on the morning of January 11th, 27-year-old Leigh Green was walking north on 7th Avenue dazed and confused. She was wearing nothing more than her bra, a long sleeved navy blue blouse cut just above the navel and her left flip flop. Her nose had bled rather severely for a while, and she had vomited twice from swallowing too much blood and drinking too much at the party she and her boyfriend had attended.

After the party, Leigh and Juan had stopped off at Mountain View Park on 7th Avenue. Juan's idea had been to feel her up while sitting in the shade of one of the trees in the park. Leigh's idea on the other hand had been to punch Juan in the mouth when he got too friendly with her. He had simply told her to get the hell out of his car before he returned her favor tenfold. She did, she wanted nothing to do with this prick Juan Martinez anymore. He tore off in his fancy new BMW (Beamer as he called it) and left her standing still fully clothed in the parking lot of the park. She did not feel well suddenly so she went in search of a bathroom. The restroom area was located only a few yards east of the parking area. She went in and the feeling of having to puke subsided, so she spritzed her face with water instead.

Leigh Green had only time to think of how bad the evening had turned out to be, when 3 white men with shaved heads walked in and pulled hunting knives on her. She asked them what they wanted and the tallest one answered "You". She didn't remember much of what else occurred because one of the men went around behind her and hit her over the head with a small club. When Leigh awoke she realized she had been raped. The men were gone, thankfully. She was lying on her back in a spread eagle position. She had swallowed a lot of blood and when she rolled over to get up she suddenly threw up a big mess of reddish brown liquid onto the floor of the women's restroom. When she felt better she peeked out of the doorway, saw that it was safe (that is she saw no one out in the park) and proceeded to go out and look for a cop and report what had happened to her. It was a very dark night and it seemed unusually still, but despite this she set out toward home and safety anyway.

The shadows along the east side of 7th Avenue seemed to shift and loom out towards her. She felt the cold cut through to the bone and she wasn't sure it was just the air temperature either. One of the shadows seemed to be moving, she turned toward the movement, nothing. She stayed there peering into the darkness waiting to see if the movement would happen again. Still nothing, but she sensed rather than saw something there just out of her sight, something dark and moving, watching her. She ran and ran, she didn't want to see what was in the bushes and the darkness waiting for and watching her. She turned left on Peoria from 7th Avenue and disappeared into the night.

The following evening. It was a cool evening, that is pleasantly cool, and the man was sitting in his home in Moon Valley only a couple miles from Mountain View Park watching some television. Kitty, his cat, was sitting next to him on the recliner when his dog (in the back yard) started to bark insanely. He decided to check it out. The back door leading to the back yard was open. "Strange" he said out loud as if someone was there to hear him. He closed and locked the door and soon forgot the matter entirely. The lock didn't always catch completely. The man's house was typical of Arizona homes. An open 2 car garage with a shed and a side door leading directly into the kitchen (normal in every way). A small front porch with a front door and a hedge mostly blocking the view of the door and the picture window. Inside was the living room (where the man sat with Kitty and occasionally his fiancée Brenda). Straight back from the front door was the kitchen, there was a hall leading to the right which led to the bathroom. Almost straight back but a little off to the left a child's bedroom, and another bedroom off to the right, and 2 closets and a pantry. Going back through the kitchen was the den (which he used mainly for storage at the moment) and the laundry room (with the back door which had stood open when he himself had not opened it), and down the hall to the right was the master bedroom (where he personally chased Kitty when he was playing with her). The man wondered briefly to himself if the wind had maybe kicked up just enough to have pushed the door open (it had happened before). The man now walking from the living room to the kitchen to get himself a beer from the refrigerator, sees Kitty, gives her the look of mock fear, reaches his hands in the air and hooks them into claws and when she returns the look (signaling play) the man then shouts "RAAHHR" and AHH the games afoot.

Kitty then proceeds to run into his bedroom and hide either behind the bed or in the closet. Kitty decides to hide at the foot of the man's bed behind the dresser and is suddenly frozen in terror right where she happens to be hiding.

Peering out from the closet door are a pair of eyes. Slitted like the eyes of a cat but horizontally rather than vertically, the pupil blue black in color and the eyes a bright shiny sickly green. Kitty just stayed put while her master continued to advance into the room unaware of the new and real danger. Kitty probably would have yelled "RUN" if she could have, but here of course that was not an option. So the man continued to enter the room containing Kitty and their new found intruder in the closet.

Movement from the closet!!! Kitty hissed as fiercely as possible (which wasn't much) and retreated to further safety. The man bewildered knelt to see what in the hell had gotten into Kitty all of a sudden (he was currently in front of the open closet). "Kitty, come here Kitty Kitty, in as soothing a voice as possible. Kitty responded to this by hissing once again and further retreating behind the dresser. The man suddenly becoming aware of danger, smelling rotten meat, turned toward the open closet door. He caught a brief glimpse of something blacker than true darkness and those damn eyes. It occurred to the man (just before the creature tore his head off that is) that he had read about this "Night Thing" in the local paper, and then of course he knew no more.

After a brief silence, the night thing then reached out of the closet, snatched up the man's body, took it into the closet with It, slammed the door shut and began to feed.

A seemingly eternal silence then followed. Kitty realizing this might be her chance for escape then darted out from behind the dresser and never looked back. Mercifully the back door had blown open this time. She would climb out through the gate to safety. And as for her master...

A NIGHT TO REMEMBER

by

William Van Parys III

One night a man and woman, after having rather hot and steamy sex, fell asleep together in the nude. Sometime during the night they both were awakened suddenly. They were dressed and sitting with their backs to each other. On the floor they sat, knees drawn up, arms resting across their knees in a large mostly dark room. They stood up, brushed off their pants (the floor was dirty) and stared at one another incredulously. The pair then checked their pockets, where they found an interesting array of items. The man found a Zippo in his left rear pocket, a torch in his right, in both front pockets he found boxes of very unusual ammunition (large caliber as well as rounds that felt rubbery to the touch). On his left hip hung a large caliber revolver that he believed to be a Colt Single Action Army or "Peace Maker" as they have been called. The gun was set in an "Old West" style holster. He took the gun out of the holster to examine it. It was not the usual old fashion style gun; it was noticeably different. It was a twelve shooter not the usual six, full metal jacket and ready to fire. In the breast pockets of the woman's button down style business shirt there was a pen in the left pocket and a pad of paper in the right. They each took stock of their possessions and began searching their surroundings.

The room they were in was enormous, the ceiling so high they were not even able to see it. When the woman first awoke she saw two doors in the wall facing her, one at each end of the wall and one door to her left. The man saw three doors all grouped together to the left side of the wall in front of him, and then noticed two more doors grouped together on the right side of the wall to his left. The man lit the torch with the lighter and they checked all the doors and noticed three of them were blocked off. The three blocked doors were obstructed by painted material, painted in fact to look like tunnels. The material seemed to be some sort of membrane.

With pen and pad in hand the woman kept track of the status of each door, so as not to become lost. The pair elected to go through one of the three doors grouped together. The door they decided upon was the one on the right. They did not notice the hieroglyphics over the door they went through. The man carried the gun in his left hand and the torch in his right as they proceeded through the tunnel.

An untold number of hours later as they were still traveling down the tunnel they happened across many strange humanoid skeletons hanging from the wall apparently chained up many years before for some unknown and unknowable crimes. The corpses extended as far as the eye could see.

Thirty minutes later as they were walking along there was a sudden change in the walls of the tunnel. The walls became alive with scenes of torture and other unspeakable apparitions. The visions all appeared to be projected on the walls, but no projection device was in evidence. Ghostly visions climbed up and over the roof of the tunnel. When it became apparent they were not prepared to attack, the man touched the wall with the barrel of the gun and noticed the wall was spongy feeling. The walls then began to bleed. The blood ran onto the floor and started to run together to form one big puddle. The large puddle began to run serpentine fashion after the man and woman, chasing them the rest of the way down the tunnel. When they reached the end, a door slid shut behind them trapping them in another room. The blood slid under the door into the room with them, and before they could move it slid toward them divided into two and slid around the two and stopped a few feet behind them. The two turned in unison and stared in amazement. Two blood beasts had changed into mirror images of themselves. The blood creatures attacked the pair. Their eyes were blood red orbs, their teeth razor sharp fangs and they immediately fell upon the hapless pair. The man fired eight or nine times at the two and either missed or the shots had no effect on the creatures. The doubles fell upon the terrified two with lightning speed. The last thing the man saw before screaming himself into wakefulness was his twin telling him not to wake up. The man awoke screaming next to his wife who was also screaming. Both were as nude as they had been upon falling asleep in each other's arms, and they soon realized they had both had the same nightmare.

After comforting each other, they showered together. During the shower the man stepped out of the shower to get another bar of soap. He walked to the sink, took a bar out of one of the drawers, looked up at the mirror, dropped the soap and screamed. Rather than seeing his own reflection in the mirror he saw his twin from the dream standing there fully clothed, eyes blood red orbs and fangs rather than teeth.

The mirror man told him to look in the cupboard below the sink and that he would know what to do with whatever he found there. Under the sink he found the gun from the "Dream", he took the revolver and turned and fired the last three of four shots at what he saw. He had shot his wife in the chest, and she fell out of the shower to the floor. She said "don't believe everything you see" and died.

At the trial he was found not guilty by reason of insanity after telling his story and was promptly institutionalized. Three years later he had been transferred to another facility. One morning he came awake suddenly, walked to the mirror and saw the spirit of his wife. She said "You know what to do now" and he did. He punched the mirror with his right fist, picked up a large chunk of the glass and slit his throat. Two hours later he was found dead of blood loss due to the gaping wound in his throat.

The staff had a mystery to solve. The man had cut his throat with a sharp object, but no such object was found and there were two sets of footprints leading out the door and down the hall, and out the doors. The doors at the end of the hall were locked and had been for some fifty years.

MOGOLLON

by
William Van Parys III

The state of Arizona is divided into 3 geographical zones. By far the most expansive of these is the desert zone, taking up almost half of the state. The next zone upward going north is the mountainous zone containing the state's largest and oldest forests. North of the mountains is the plateau zone containing some of the oldest Indian tribes. On the southern edge of the plateau (running roughly two hundred miles along the edge of the plateau) is what is known to all of the locals as the Mogollon Rim.

Some of the strangest tales I have ever heard come from this area north of most of the main metropolitan areas. Tales of all sorts of magic ranging from good to very bad. Of UFO's and monster sightings of all kinds, of deities (mainly evil) sweeping down on the stranded or lonely passerby in the middle of a dark night, particularly on the main highway leading from Phoenix to Heber, a dark and lonely road where the trees seem to loom over the road, and staring at the monotony of them leads to all sorts of tricks of the eye, or maybe not.

It is on this lonely stretch of road I now travel, listening to some bad ass jams on the radio, namely an old Black Sabbath tape of mine, trying desperately not to look at the trees, which seem to get closer to me all the time. Only a few minutes ago the song Black Sabbath (creepy as all hell on the right or wrong occasions if you prefer) was playing full blast when I happened to glance off to my right, for no apparent reason, and thought that I saw the green faced witch like woman that is on the cover of that now rather ancient album. I hit the accelerator with both feet so hard, my feet went numb seconds later, just to get out of there as fast as I could.

I am supposed to be going hunting with some buddies of mine up along the Mogollon Rim. Snipe hunting is what my friend Jorge Rojas told me, but what the hell does he know anyway, he's just a dickhead. He may be a peckerhead, but he is my best friend. He doesn't have to worry about being home anytime soon, because he recently divorced his wife Marjorie and anyway who gives a wad? Marjorie was a slut from the word go.

There are five in all of us going on the hunting trip. We are actually going deer hunting, not snipe hunting. The five going on the trip are, Jorge Rojas, Clyde Nesmith (the crazy old fart), Norman Jones (the dork of the group), Pete Souther, and myself John Reece. Myself I am soon to be married to my fiancée Suzy Koontz (putting it mildly in other words, I have only a few days and certainly no more than a week).

For firepower we would be carrying the following, Jorge has his twelve-gauge shotgun, Clyde his old Winchester shotgun, Norman his twenty-two rifle as well as his Ruger twenty-two semi-automatic pistol with two nine round clips reserve (three clips total in all), Pete his 30-30 and of course I myself will be bringing my 30-30, my .38 revolver and of course my baby a Blackhawk .357 magnum with hollow point shells (just in case things get a little carried away). Not that I am paranoid or anything like that, but sometimes more than one weapon is required for the job. Heh-heh-heh!

Upon my arrival at the spot where we would be camping I discovered that I was once again the very last one to show up. Naturally enough I suppose they all had to start dogging on me in turn. First as usual was Pete. "Late as usual Dumb Ass" was Pete's usual comment, and this time was no disappointment. "Fuck you, Shirley" was my usual come back and as well I did not disappoint him either.

Clyde's comment was weird as usual, "Hey John, Confuscious say "Man who walk through subway turnstyle sideways going to bang cock" whatever the hell that had to do with me being late the crazy old bastard. Clyde Nesmith had a way of saying things which did not make any sense and if they did (and this is a big IF) you still had to be wondering what he had been drinking earlier that day.

We decided to load all of our things into the little shack we would be using for the trip that night. We would be getting up around 3am the following morning, to get as early a start as possible. We would each be carrying a pack filled with the things we might need out in the field. Canned goods, some utensils, napkins, toilet paper extra ammo, shit like that you see just in case we were gone longer than we planned to be, or simply got lost perhaps.

On the first day out we saw only one deer, and that happened to be a foal. On the second day out we saw a group of three deer one of which was a legal kill. Norman and Pete each took a shot at the one and missed. Norm dropped his gun, the gun went off hitting a branch high above the deer, the branch then fell and hit the adult female deer in the head sending her into an unplanned nap. We proceeded to leave that area as quickly as possible.

Norman Jones has an ass roughly the size of Mt. Mingus (only a few miles west of here) and that was evident when he tried to put his gun belt on. He had the belt specially made because he was too big for most gun belts. Norm was a pretty smart guy for the most part, but he sure was one clumsy dude. If there were some stupid accident, he could have Norm would figure it out.

Day three was completely uneventful, besides of course the time Pete saw a bush overloaded with some kind of berries, ate one (remarking how good they were) and immediately puked it back up, the dumb shit. Sometimes Pete could be a real moron, today was no exception. The third day quickly turned into the third night out. When it did we suddenly discovered we were very lost. Of course Clyde decided he needed to take a major dump so he took his pack in hand and tromped off to the bushes, announcing to the world "time for my daily dump."

Clyde returned from his adventure white faced and out of breath for some unknown reason. Pete said "Must have been one hell of a shit to have that sort of reaction. What did you do? Fall in?" "No you dumb asshole but you should see what I saw on the other side of those berry bushes." Clyde remarked. I said "What, a ghost or a werewolf!" "Ha ha isn't that really fuckin' funny!?" Clyde scoffed. (Not really meant as as a question at all). "Well get your guns and your packs and follow me. This must be one hell of an animal." Clyde stated. Pete replied "Ah come on guys, let's eat first, then we'll go check out Clyde's hallucinations after."

Later we followed Clyde, though none of us were really interested in what Clyde described as one hell of an animal. He said on the way there that whatever it was had killed many large animals which included, elk, deer, wolves, javelina, and ominously enough bear (namely grizzlies, it appeared.)

When I saw the carnage of years (maybe even centuries of slaughter) I swallowed hard and fumbled for something to say. Finally I looked around and saw that everyone else was having the same problem I was, in short, wanting to get the fuck out of there now!

Finally, Jorge managed "This is a very bad place guys, I don't like this one fuckin' bit. Let's get the hell out of here and screw the rest of the hunting trip."

I said to Jorge "Look man over there that cave is big enough for something much larger than a bear to live in." "I know that, shut the fuck up I didn't want to think about that." Jorge countered.

As the night got darker and darker we made our way back in the direction we thought might be camp. It turned out we were just going in circles, and we REALLY did not want that.

By midnight we had finally managed to make some headway, some I suppose is better than none. We decided (with considerable reluctance of course) to make camp. This turned out to be the "Queen Mother" of all mistakes, of course, but it seemed like the best idea at the time. We ended up camping at the foot of the very hill where we had found the large cave (simply put we were back at square one, only this time we were on the other side of it).

It was starting to get light, just a little bit anyway, in the eastern sky. All was so incredibly quiet it was as if someone, when we weren't looking, had swooped down while we were sleeping and took all of the wildlife away. Not the call of a Mourning Dove, or the cry of a coyote, or any one of perhaps a myriad of other sounds were to be heard. Needless to say that was disquieting as hell and we could do nothing but sit and wait and see if something happened or not. Inevitably something terrible eventually did, but for the moment all was quiet.

Norman decided it was time to squeeze the juice off of his lemon and proceeded to round the hill. It was still quite dark out and still had that too quiet "feel" to it when Norm came running around the hill at roughly the speed of light. I have never seen such a fat ass as Norm Jones move so fast in my life. If the outcome had been different it would have been the funniest thing I have ever seen. It was clear that Norm had discovered who lived in the cave after all. From the look of abysmal terror on his face we knew that we were all doomed and that it was going to be a new adventure in hell before it was over. If any of us survived, we would probably have to be committed and would possibly even want to be.

The thing that chased Norm out from behind the hill looked like something out of the blackest of nightmares. It towered at somewhere between fifty and sixty feet high, it looked like a giant black blob of sludge. It also appeared to have one big eye at its center and the mouth was a gaping hole with giant fangs for teeth. It moved at an incredible rate of speed crushing trees and anything that happened to get in its way. It overtook Norman so fast that he didn't have a snowball's chance in hell. At least that's the way it appeared to me anyway.

The monster or whatever it was almost swallowed Norm whole, but it paused for effect (seemingly anyway or maybe it just appeared that way), at any rate however, it still bit him in half and then swallowed him whole. Clyde Nesmith then got behind a tree and started shooting at the creature (the only effect this had on the creature was further pissing it off), the creature then fell upon Clyde. It slammed into the tree Clyde was standing under and it immediately fell over on him, pinning him to the ground. It was by no means finished with him. It bit at him (killing him instantly when it did), scooping up not only Clyde, but a terrified squirrel and a huge chunk of the tree itself. This left just Pete, Jorge and myself to get the hell out of there.

After only a few minutes which seemed like years, we finally found the trail we were looking for and still the creature seemed to be following us. It followed us back to the little cottage we were staying in during our hunting trip.

When we returned to camp, Jorge pulled his twelve gauge (which he had forgotten to take with him) from the back of his truck. It was already loaded, so he didn't have to worry about trying to load it cock it and still fire upon the creature before it attacked. He immediately opened fire upon the creature, succeeded in slowing it momentarily and then had to reload while Pete and I tried to at least slow it down enough to get in our trucks and make like a tree and leave. We held the creature off a little, but not enough.

Finally, it seemed to get bored with this game and rushed us faster than we could blink. It first slammed through both Clyde's and Norm's trucks, pushing them into Pete's and then into Jorge's. Jorge was caught between his and Pete's truck killing him almost instantly. Pete and I were planning to make a break for my truck when it started after us. We flanked around the beast, amazingly enough we actually got to my truck,started it and got the fuck out of there. We could see it fading away behind us, we hoped that it would not follow us.

Amazingly enough we actually managed to escape that scene with our lives. But as we drove on (down the creepy Beeline Highway, of all places) toward the Phoenix metropolitan area, strange and ominous reports of a giant blob like creature began pouring in from many of the small outlying towns, headed in the direction of the densely populated Phoenix area.

We could only hope they would evacuate Phoenix before the so called "Mogollon Monster" came to call on the millions of residents there.

Sylvia

By

William Van Parys III

One night as I was driving north on Cave Creek Rd., I noticed a young woman standing along the shoulder thumbing for a ride. I stopped a hundred feet or so ahead of her and leaned over and opened the car door. "Thanks" she said walking up to the car, "no problem, where ya headed" I said as she cautiously slipped into the passenger seat. "I really appreciate this. It seems like I've been walking for years" she said. Quickly she added. "You're not a psycho murderer or anything are you?" "I haven't killed anyone lately; I'm trying to cut back." She cackled at that, a rather unsettling sound.

At that point I noticed she was an incredibly beautiful blonde with the greenest eyes I had ever seen. She was wearing a dark gray velour blouse with sleeves that ended just below the elbow, a black leather skirt that was cut too high to be legal and dark gray sandals.

"So what can I call you beautiful?" I asked her. "Sylvia" she replied. "Well Sylvia, where can I leave you off at?" I asked. "You can drop me off at the house at the end of the canal road" she said. I noticed she was staring at me intensely. While she was staring at me, I began to become uncomfortable with the look she was giving me.

"Would you mind if I slipped off my shoes?" she asked. "Not at all, make yourself comfortable" I said a little too emphatically. I got a real good look at just how lovely her legs were when she put her feet up on the dashboard. I noticed her toenails were painted a deep scarlet color as were her fingernails and full voluptuous lips. She was looking at me as if she wanted me to play with her legs, and I was most happy to oblige. From there it seemed we came to her house at the end of the small canal road. She jumped out and thanked me for the ride. Then she ran around behind the house without another word, and I drove away.

I had the weekend off. Saturday afternoon I went shopping and bought a few items that I needed. That night I went to a party at a friend's house, drank a little too much and after the party I called a cab. During the course of the cab ride home I thought about Sylvia the pretty blonde from the night before. She had done something to me the night before I was sure of it.

Sunday came and went with nothing more than taking the bus over to my friend's house to pick up my car.

It was Monday evening after work I noticed that Sylvia had forgotten her sandals. I decided to go home and have dinner and watch some television. Later that night I would take her shoes back and apologize for not reminding her of them in the first place.

On the way back to her house late that night (I had fallen asleep in front of the television set), I remembered the way she had stared at me, and shivered. There was something in her eyes that really bothered me. Touching Sylvia's leg somehow in some way erased my memory. I had no recollection of anything until I pulled up in front of her house. At that point I pulled up in the circular driveway and noticed the house (or whatever it was) had the unmistakable air of being abandoned. I reached over and picked up her sandals. I stepped out onto the asphalt drive and started toward the house. I figured I would knock on the door and leave her shoes on the front porch.

I got to the door, dropped the sandals to the right of the door and knocked. I turned and started away when the door suddenly opened a few inches. There was no one inside the door that I could see and no one reached out to grab the shoes. In my mind's eye I saw her standing behind the door. I went back to the door, I decided I really did not want to see her, but when I tried to stop myself I found that I couldn't and continued forward. When I reached out to push open the door (I couldn't stop my hand either) a scaly hand with claws on it grabbed my arm and yanked me into the darkness. Cat's eyes stared out of the darkness into my own. It reached out with its claws and tore my throat out. The last thought that went through my head was I'm leaking, and then I knew nothing more.

The scaly hand reached out the door, took the sandals, pulled back through the opening and closed the door.

Valley of Blood

by
William Van Parys III

While the Night Creeper was freezing his ass off in his first summer in North Carolina, a man in his early to mid-thirties was dining on the heart and liver of a homeless man.

Jeffrey Johnson finished his meal, got up and put his dishes in the sink. While running water into the sink he contemplated what parts he would consume later. Johnson was currently deciding how exactly he would emerge from the Creepers shadow. In a city this size that just didn't seem likely. He was thinking maybe he should just dump the bums body and take another.

What he didn't know was detectives Joaquin Pedersen and Dennis Dilweg were as we speak watching his apartment. Pedersen and Dilweg had been on this unnamed killer's trail since before transferring to the Flagstaff Police Department. Jeff Johnson would find that out soon enough.

It was still light out when Johnson climbed behind the wheel of his 1975 Pinto and drove away into the deepening evening. At some point Pedersen and Dilweg lost sight of the puke green car and somehow, someway the hideous green car disappeared into heavy late rush hour traffic.

At 11pm that evening Johnson found a young man jogging around a crappy little park in South Phoenix. He sat down on a bench and the young man came over and the two conversed for a few minutes. It was five minutes into the conversation when Johnson became aware that the man was gay and attracted to him. It made him very uncomfortable, but despite his discomfort he decided this man might make a good meal and therefore invited him to room with him at one of those hotels along Van Buren, and he knew just the right place indeed.

The two men entered the room, and they sat on the edge of the bed. Todd (here's a fucking surprise) began massaging Jeff's leg, that pang of discomfort again. According to the opinion of just about every profiler in the country Jeff Johnson is considered a homosexual offender. Meaning that he kills only other males. This is untrue to Johnson however; to him it is all about taking the life force of other human beings by consuming various parts of their bodies.

He wanted to play a game with the young man that the younger man may be all too familiar with. He couldn't remember the technical term for it, but the basic gist is one person will use strategic strangulation to give the partner what amounts to a kind of head rush. For some people this is a source of sexual stimulation.

Rather than strangling the man the way he wanted, he chose to break his neck instead. In a frenzy Johnson then sliced little chunks from the man's buttocks, consumed them raw and left the room. He just left the man on the bed.

Upon returning home Johnson decided to get rid of the body in his freezer. Pedersen and Dilweg were driving up just as he hauled the body around the building to be stowed in the dumpster.

Jeff Johnson is a man who acts strictly on impulse. Killing for him is always done in a frenzy. He was unaware of voices that were commanding him to act with reckless abandon. The same voices (instincts to him) were telling him to dump the frozen body as they had told him to take once victim after another.

Pedersen noted the bundle Johnson was dragging wrapped in black plastic. Dilweg had not yet noticed the unyielding package the killer was dragging. Dilweg himself was too busy worrying over a rather large burrito the way a dog would worry over a bone.

Pedersen said something unintelligible to Dilweg, and Dilweg grunted and farted loudly.

"Pay attention muthafucka!" Pedersen to Dilweg.

Dilweg to Pedersen "Bite my crank beeotch!"

With a brief grin Pedersen said "That's the worst impression of a brother I ever heard."

Dilweg made a rude gesture and went on eating.

"Listen to me, you go round to that big dumpster and wait for him there. I will come up from behind, pull my gun and get him to surrender." Pedersen said with iron resolve.

"Yeah, yeah, go fuck your mother." Dilweg replied.

"I will fuck your mother if this goes down the way I hope it does." Pedersen proclaimed.

Pedersen and Dilweg were always engaging in mock arguments like this. It helped them pass the long hours of waiting for the freaks to make their move. Whatever that may be.

Jeff Johnson was standing in front of the dumpster where he planned to deposit the body. He looked for all the world like a man receiving messages from the other side. Clearly he did not appreciate what he was hearing.

Suddenly Johnson glared at the far side of the dumpster where Detective Dilweg was crouched and ready to surprise the killer. Johnson with fearful agility leaped into the dumpster, reached over the back and yanked Dilweg up by the hair. Dilweg reached up with his gun and it was knocked away immediately. Johnson let loose with a scream of pain and rage as Pedersen pistol whipped the killer across the back of the head, and just like that Jeffrey Johnson was carted around to the trunk of their unmarked Taurus.

A sudden premonition told Pedersen to make sure the shotgun under the front seat was unlocked from its restraint. He did as his sudden insight told him. In the blink of an eye Jeff Johnson managed to break the plastic cuffs. He grabbed for Dilweg's service Glock, removed it from its holster then fired. A harmless click. He released the safety, then fired shattering Dilweg's left knee cap. Johnson turned, the butt of the shotgun caught him in the nose bringing a torrent of blood and pain that temporarily blinded him. He fired again piercing Pedersen's left ear. Pedersen fired vaporizing Johnson's right arm from the elbow down to his wrist. Johnson absently reached down with his left hand, and removed the gun from what was left of his own right hand. Pedersen tucked the barrel of the shotgun under Johnson's chin. Recognition dawned in Johnson's eyes just then. "Do it. Please do it. I don't want to kill anymore," Johnson pleaded. "Will do muthafucka." Pedersen replied as he pulled the trigger. Johnson's head disappeared in a cloud of bloody chunks that turned Pedersen's stomach threateningly.

Detective Dennis Eugene Dilweg would recover with only a minor limp. However, he would pull desk duty for the rest of his career. Which is too bad, he was a promising young field detective.

Detective Joaquin Haralder Pedersen would on occasion travel back down to Phoenix to help Fletcher down

and Walker work on the Night Creeper case. In the year 2005 he would help chase the Creeper down the 202 toward the Beeline Highway and potential freedom. The Night Creeper would look out the driver's window of the stolen cruiser and mark Pedersen with his freakishly ruined face.

GLOOM AND DOOM

by Bill Van Parys

Wh|at does it all mean?

Life has many questions with few answers.

Will there someday be answers to people's questions?

Will we be granted peace of mind, or will we be forever blind?

Pools of blood, inflicted by fools.

With many breaking life's rules.

Stop all the hate, or death will be our fate.

Once gone, it can never be retrieved.

Nothing but emptiness, and life in the past.

End all the madness, for we want no more sadness.

Is there a light at the end of this black tunnel?

Or does it end with more darkness, if it ends at all?

Hate or love, war or peace, death and destruction or life and reconstruction?

What will become our fate?

'Til the bitter end

WE WILL FIGHT TO THE DEATH!

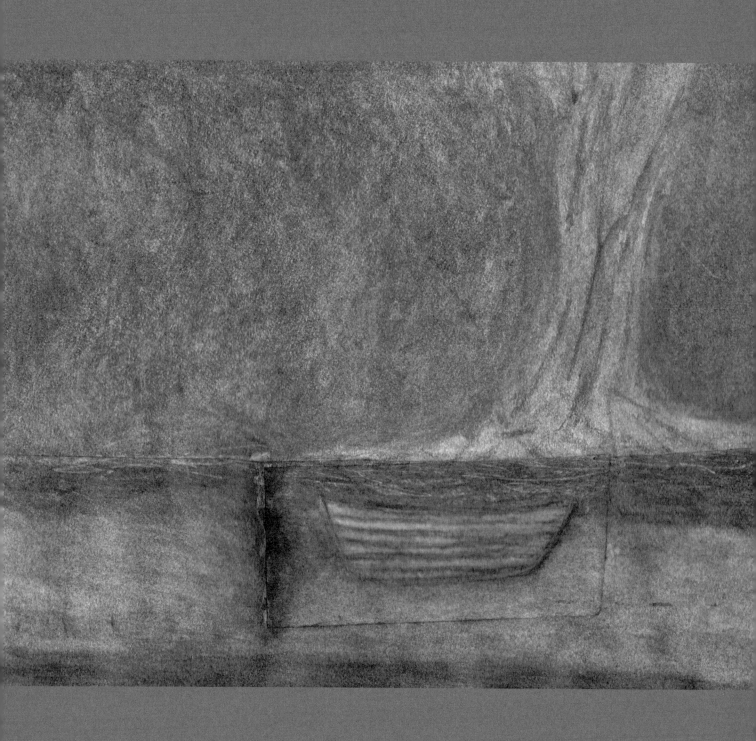

ONE DARK NIGHT

By Bill Van Parys

One dark, rainy night I found myself walking down the
deserted street to death.

The wind howled through the trees sending a chill
through my body.

The trees looked as if they were marching toward me.

I heard the scream of the banshee, I ran, tripped
and fell.

I picked myself up, but it was all over, she was
right behind me.

I know the end is near.

One dark night I fear.

FROSTY DEATH

By Bill Van Parys

Bells are ringing.
Telling you it's time to die. Yeah!
You run in every direction.
Trying to escape the fate of your own confession. Yeah!
You beg your mother
To let you play with me.
If only you knew.
Your life would come to an end. Yeah!
Take my hand my friend,
And I will lead you into darkness.
Darkness black as pitch.
But did you know, you're one dead bitch?! Yeah!
Don't hold your breath.
You're going to die a frosty death.
Coldness of death.
Stealing away your life. Yeah!
You lie in your bed.
Taken by the evil dead. Hell Yeah!

Rain and Orange Sunshine

By Bill Van Parys

All I can see is rain and orange sunshine.

Black clouds, rain, thunder and lightning,
highlight my gloomy darkness.

On that day, during the storm, you left me.
Plunging me into eternal blackness.
I lost all touch with reality.

I felt the evils of life crashing down upon me.
Slowly, day by day, tearing the life from me.

Leveled by life, I stumbled home to the
relief of my sunshine.

It seemed as if life were now coming
to an end.

Now, until my dying day, all I will ever know,
is rain and orange sunshine.

THE SHELL

By Willam A. Van Parys III

A seashell on the beach that is the world.

A world filled with Life.

A world filled with Strife.

A world filled with Happiness.

A world filled with Darkness.

These are the things that make me Not want to open the door.

To the world no more.

This is the world of the Shell.

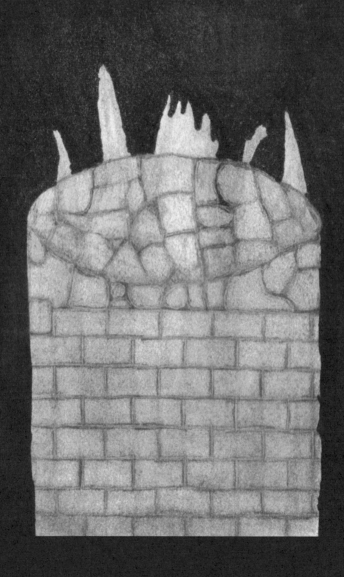

THE WELL TO HELL

by Bill Van Parys

There I stood in front of the large black house, dark as hell.
I heard a noise, I turned to see a mouse fall into the well.
The Well to Hell
Oh Hell
I opened the door and I looked inside.
As I looked, there were many doors off the the side.
I opened the third door,
There I saw Her with the fangs of a boar.
I ran out,
She smiled at me with Her fangs out.
I know that I couldn't get away,
But still I ran 'til the end of day.
I stumbled and fell,
I looked up, there was the well.
The house in the day, blackened by hate.
I ran 'til I had come upon my fate.
There stood the lady with the fangs of a boar.
She had lived a life of absolute gore.
The Well to Hell
All's Not Well

Into the will I fell back,
Until I felt my head crack.
I struggled to get away,
I knew I would never see the light of day.

The Will to Hell
Oh Bloody Hell

The Well to Hell
All's Not Well

The Well to Hell
Oh Please Don't Take Me Hell!

Who Goes There?

By Bill Van Parys

Mysterious shadows in the night.
Walking through darkness of no light.
Entering a night of no end.
Full of hate and bent revenge.
The dark figure will avenge.
Coming upon the enemies door
there stood the figure of an evil whore.
Blackened by hate of merciless fate.
The figure stood tall and straight.
The whore turned and ran from the door.
Through the gate went the whore.
It was too late
to escape her own fate.

Printed in the United States
By Bookmasters